Ashley Baxendale & Anna Kukleva

FISHING for CONDIMENTS

TINY TREE

TINY TREE

Fishing for Condiments
Published in 2025 by
Tiny Tree Books
West Wing Studios
Unit 166, The Mall
Luton, LU1 2TL
tinytreebooks.com

On the frozen lake nothing stirred.
Neget's mind kept returning to the kitchen at home.

Waiting for him there were cupboards brimming with his favourite condiments, yet each cupboard was empty of fish.

“I know what you’re thinking,” said Grandpa gently.

Even though Grandpa’s face was covered from the biting wind, Neget knew that Grandpa was smiling.

"Buy a man a fish and you feed him for a day;

teach a man to fish and you feed him for a lifetime," Grandpa continued.

Without a day's catch, Neget's belly grumbled.

“All these sauces at home without a single fish,” they heard it say.

The sky began to bruise as the hour grew late.
It felt like all their hard work had been for nothing.

“We don’t have anything to eat tonight, do we?” Neget asked.

“Not yet,” Grandpa replied.

The ice crunched softly as Grandpa knelt down,
"I'll join you back at camp," he said.
"Look after this Neget, it's all we have."

In the growing darkness Neget walked back to camp
and Grandpa disappeared into the distance.

For the first time, Neget felt alone.

Inside the hut, the loneliness grew and grew. As he sat on the bed, Neget remembered what Grandpa had given him on the ice.

Unfolding a black and white photograph, he saw Grandpa, only as tall as Neget, from another time.

If Neget could have given all the condiments in all the cupboards of the world for Grandpa to return, he would have.

As he sat on the bed, only the ticking of the clock and the crackle of the fire broke the silence.

But then the wooden door suddenly burst open.
Grandpa stood smiling with his prize high in the air.

"There's even enough to share!" he exclaimed proudly.

As they walked home, Neget felt closer to Grandpa than ever before. “What use are all your favourite sauces if you don’t have any fish?” he asked aloud.

Without answering, Grandpa turned to Neget and smiled his familiar smile.

For Ada
The sea in the sky,
The sand under the sea.

Ashley Baxendale

To those days when I was
young enough to know the truth

Anna Kukleva

www.ingramcontent.com/pod-product-compliance
Ingram Content Group UK Ltd.
Pitfield, Milton Keynes, MK11 3LW, UK
UKRC031122200125
453746UK00009B/33

9781837918799